CHADWICK

and the

Garplegrungen

By

Priscilla Cummings

Illustrated by A.R. Cohen

Tidewater Publishers
Centreville, Maryland

Chadwick never tired of being a star at the big, beautiful aquarium in Baltimore. Even if he was just a common blue crab from the Chesapeake Bay, people still crowded around his tank to watch him swim upside down and snap his claws.

But, truth be known, Chadwick did get a little homesick now and then. So, one day when a letter postmarked Shady Creek drifted down through the water to him, he eagerly snatched it up and began to read:

Dear Chadwick,

Matilda is terribly sick and you know what a stubborn old egret she is. She just won't listen to anyone's advice.

Not only that, but Orville the Oyster's Uncle Rockefeller was robbed of all his pearls last night and there wasn't a thing to be done because the entire Bluefish Patrol is out sick, too.

It's serious, Chadwick. Matilda might not last if we don't help her. Can you come?

Your friend,
Bernie the Sea Gull

It didn't take Chadwick long to make up his mind. Of course he would go home!

Chadwick knew if he ever needed to get out of the aquarium fast all he needed to do was pull the plug on the drain in his tank. Then he could zip right out through one of the pipes, which emptied into the harbor. From there, he'd have to make the long swim home, down the river and across the Chesapeake Bay.

With one strong yank he pulled the drain stopper and—WHOOSH!—out he went. The water was cold but a small vest and lots of fast swimming kept Chadwick warm.

When he arrived back at Shady Creek, Bernie greeted him with a loud squawk. "Gosh, am I glad to see you, Chadwick! Quick, come see Matilda."

Chadwick followed as they stepped carefully through the tall marsh grass so as not to startle Matilda, who was lying on her back with her eyes closed. Her reading glasses rested on her chest and she was so feverish that the three flowers in her pillbox hat drooped.

"Matilda," Chadwick whispered, "Can you hear me?"

Slowly, she opened her eyes and turned to squint at the crab. "Chadwick?" She smiled faintly. "Thank you for coming, but there's nothing to be done for me now. It's just a matter of time, I'm afraid."

"Don't give up so easily," Chadwick insisted. "We'll get Dr. Mallard! He's a smart duck!"

Matilda's eyes opened wide and she tried to sit up. "You're not bringing Dr. Mallard to see me—not that old quack!"

"Oh, come now, Matilda. Dr. Mallard's no quack. Why, one summer when my shell peeled off too fast and I caught a cold, he fixed me up in no time."

Bernie chuckled. "You sure looked funny, Chadwick, wearing that big sweater until your new shell grew on."

While Bernie flew off to fetch the doctor, Chadwick piled some blankets on Matilda and tried to make her more comfortable. "You'll be all right," he reassured her as he untied her hat and hung it on a nearby reed.

Dr. Mallard was so fat he was easy to spot as he appeared low in the sky. He braced his wide webbed feet for a splashy landing in Shady Creek and then waddled ashore, coughing and quacking.

First, he took Matilda's temperature and listened to her heart. Then he looked into her near-sighted eyes and examined her long throat. It seemed to take forever, but Dr. Mallard always did things at his own slow pace.

"Well, what do you think, Doctor?" Chadwick asked anxiously. "Will she be okay?"

"I'm afraid it doesn't look good," Dr. Mallard said as he closed up his black bag. "About all you can do is keep her warm and offer her some fish broth." He reached for his pocket watch. "It's getting late. I must fly along. I've got to check on the Bluefish Patrol."

"But wait a minute—what's wrong with everyone?" Chadwick asked.

"B-a-a-a-a-a-d stomach aches," Dr. Mallard said. "And there's nothing I can do."

Chadwick was shocked. "Do you know what's causing these stomach aches?" he asked.

"Of course," Dr. Mallard said matter-of-factly. "The garplegrungen."

"Garple—what?!" Bernie and Chadwick asked.

"Garplegrungen. It rhymes with dungeon," said Dr. Mallard. "Come on, I'll show you." He shook his tail as he turned. With Bernie and Chadwick following, the doctor waddled back down to the shoreline, where he stopped, planting his big feet in the sand. "See all this . . . *stuff*?"

Chadwick and Bernie stared at the green and purple bubbles that came ashore with each gentle lapping of the waves.

"Yuck," said Chadwick. "What *is* that?"

"Garplegrungen," said Dr. Mallard.

Chadwick frowned. "What's it made of? Where does it come from?"

"I don't know," Dr. Mallard said, shrugging. "But it's going to make us all sick if we don't get rid of it."

Chadwick snapped his claws angrily. "Then we will get rid of it!" he declared.

Dr. Mallard and Bernie turned silently to look at

Chadwick. Neither one of them had any idea how to rid the entire Chesapeake Bay of the awful garplegrungen. Chadwick knew it would be up to him to find a way.

*   *   *

"The first thing we need is some good advice," Chadwick decided. "What about Toulouse? We could ask—"

"Don't bother with him!" Bernie interrupted. "He's just one highfalutin French Canada goose now. Ever since his cooking school opened, he hasn't had time for old friends."

"We've got to try," Chadwick urged.

"If you say so. But don't expect much," Bernie warned. Reluctantly, he took off for the long flight to Blackwater Refuge, where Toulouse was vacationing with thousands of other geese for the winter.

Chadwick waved good-bye, then swam off to the deep and warmer water at the bottom of the bay, where the boy crabs napped during the cold weather.

"Wake up, Pincher Pete! Rise and shine, Bug-Eyed Benny! I need your help!" Chadwick hollered as he thumped on the sleeping crabs with his claws and kicked up mud with his swimming legs.

"OUCH! STOP THAT!" came a sharp cry from a voice Chadwick didn't recognize. "Can't you do what you're seeing? I . . . I mean, can't you see what you're doing?"

Chadwick gasped and darted to one side. He didn't realize he had been jumping on top of Belly Jeans the Flounder.

"I'm *so* sorry," Chadwick said. "But gee whiz, Belly Jeans, you always lie so flat on the bottom no one can see you."

"Don't apologize," Belly Jeans said as he shook the sand off his back. "I'm always getting stepped on. Seems I'm not anything for good. That is to say, I'm not good for anything."

"Oh, come now," Chadwick said. "You're always putting yourself down. I didn't mean to jump on you—

honest! And look, I'm sure you're good for something—even if you do get things backwards." Chadwick stopped to think. "Listen, Belly Jeans, maybe you could help me wake up the crabs. I need their help to get rid of the garplegrungen."

Belly Jeans turned his eyes downward. "I'm sorry, Chadwick, but I can't help you get the bed out of crabs. Er . . . get the crabs out of bed. I'm so dumb that sometimes I can't even wake myself up."

It was hard to cheer up a flounder who always felt sorry for himself.

Miles away, Bernie was gliding down from the sky in a wide circle, searching for a place to land at Blackwater Refuge. The field below him resembled an enormous family reunion with hundreds of French Canada geese snacking on corn and honking as they walked around visiting one another. In perfect "V" formation, gaggles flew in and out.

"Can someone help me?" Bernie shouted above all the noise as his feet touched down. "I'm looking for Toulouse!"

"He's down by the pond—sulking," said one of the geese.

Bernie was confused. "Why's he so gloomy? I thought he was the big shot around here now with that silly cooking school of his."

The geese nearby grew quiet. "Didn't you hear?" one of them asked. "He had to close down the cooking school. The water went bad when that awful garplegrungen got into it."

"Oh dear," said Bernie. He turned and walked briskly toward the pond, where he found Toulouse sitting by a log.

At first Toulouse didn't even lift his head. "It was so very terrible," he said, sniffing. "The popovers—they wouldn't pop over. And all the French pastry turned out green and purple."

Even Bernie—who ate just about anything—shuddered when he heard that. "We must get rid of the garplegrungen, Toulouse! It made Matilda sick and now it's ruined your cook-ing school."

Toulouse looked sadly at Bernie. "You know," he said, "I've been so worried about my own problems, I haven't been a very good friend, eh? Why, I didn't even know Matilda was sick." Toulouse thought for a moment, then pushed his big round belly up off the ground. His eyes sparkled with the excitement of a great idea. "Come with me, mon ami! Come with me, my friend!"

"Where are we going?" Bernie asked as they flew off together.

"To the marsh!" Toulouse yelled against the wind. "We'll ask Baron von Heron where the garplegrungen comes from! He'll know!"

Bernie had never met the Baron, but he'd heard all about the great blue heron who was taller than seven sea gulls stacked one on the other. Baron von Heron was such a noble bird he didn't speak in mere sentences, he always talked in rhyme. And when you spoke to the Baron, Bernie was told, you always addressed him as Your Birdship.

The Baron was standing knee-deep in the water when Bernie and Toulouse splashed down. Bernie couldn't get over how long and curved the Baron's neck was, nor how skinny his royal legs.

"We're sorry to bother you, Your Birdship," Toulouse said. "But we need to know where the garplegrungen comes from. It's making everyone sick and it's ruined my cooking school."

Baron von Heron paused and took a long look at Toulouse through his monocle. He cleared his long throat—"ahem!"—then, slowly, he spoke:

"So, you're the bird of which I heard.
A *cooking school*—my, how absurd!"

Toulouse was embarrassed. "Well, maybe it was not such a good idea, eh? But about the garplegrungen, Your Birdship. Do you know where it comes from?"

Baron von Heron took a deep breath and gazed off toward a distant shoreline before answering.

"Oh yes, of course. Indeed I do.
It's as obvious as my feathers are blue.
I tell you this, with some distaste:
the garplegrungen comes from people waste.
It's fertilizer from their lands,
and trash they've thrown out with their hands.
It's junk from factories, gunk from farms.
People don't realize how many things it harms.
They think these green and purple bubbles
are someone else's ugly troubles.
Pollution they call it. I call it a shame!
It's people—my dear friends—people are to blame!"

Bernie and Toulouse listened carefully.

"I should have known it was people. Sometimes they don't stop to think what they're doing," said Toulouse.

Bernie's thick eyebrows came together as he tried to think. "What in the world can we do?"

The Baron's reply was quick and simple:

"The solution to pollution
is to stop its distribution."

Toulouse beamed. "That's it! We shall stop the garplegrungen from coming into the water!"

"I can't wait to tell Chadwick!" Bernie squawked.

As the Baron watched the two birds fly off in a frenzy of flapping wings, a shadow fell over his face. He knew they were in for an unpleasant surprise.

*   *   *

By the time the birds returned to Shady Creek, so had Chadwick's girlfriend, Esmerelda. Chadwick didn't realize how much he had missed her until he saw her curly crab eyelashes again. "I have something to ask you, but it will have to wait until later," he whispered to her as he held her claw.

Turning back to the others, Chadwick said in a loud voice, "Okay. We know the garplegrungen is pollution. On my way home from Baltimore I saw a drain pipe that was dumping garplegrungen into the Bay. We'll gather up empty oyster shells, some rocks and dried grass and block up that pipe. In the meantime, Bernie, you bottle up the garplegrungen in Shady Creek. Goodness knows you've picked up enough empty soda bottles. Now you finally have a use for them!"

Chadwick and Esmerelda gathered everything and piled it onto an old fish net. It was a long haul, but the two small crabs dragged the net all the way to the drain pipe, where Toulouse and Dr. Mallard were waiting to help.

They worked for hours. Just when Dr. Mallard stuffed
what he thought was the last hunk of grass in the pipe,
a gush of dirty water burst through, soaking him from head
to webbed foot. "Now look what's happened!" he wailed.
"Stinky garplegrungen all over!"

"I see something worse than that," said Toulouse.
"Look past that sailboat. There are three more pipes dumping
garplegrungen!"

"Yes—and see the oily water running off that parking
lot?!" Esmerelda moaned. She put her pincers over her
eyes and drifted to the bottom in defeat.

Chadwick followed her. "Let's go home, Esmerelda.
We'll think of something else." He tried to sound encourag-
ing, but his voice was weary.

By the time Chadwick and the others returned, Bernie
was filling his last empty soda bottle. "What do I do
now?" he asked, wiping the sweat off his brow. Behind
him, lined along a stand of marsh grass, was a long row
of bottles, each filled with green and purple liquid. "I'm
out of bottles and there's still lots of garplegrungen left."

"Forget it," said Dr. Mallard, as he shook his wet
pocket watch and held it to his ear. "It's no use. I tried
to tell you there was nothing we can do."

Chadwick sighed. "Let's all take a break. I, for one,
am starving and would like to eat some eel grass."

"Eel grass? There isn't any eel grass around here,"
said Matilda, who huddled nearby, shivering under a
blanket. "The garplegrungen destroyed that, too."

Chadwick was really angry now. "That does it!" he shouted. "We'll just have to think of some other way to get rid of the garplegrungen!"

Toulouse suggested that Orville's rich Uncle Rockefeller Oyster could pay to have the garplegrungen removed. But who would he pay to remove it?

Esmerelda suggested they all pack up and move out into the ocean. But the ocean was too salty for some of them, too cold for the others. Besides, the Chesapeake Bay was their home. Why should they have to move?

Although the others didn't know it, Baron von Heron had been standing behind them, listening. He cleared his throat—"ahem!"—and stepped forward to speak.

"I'm afraid the doctor's right.
This is something you can't fight.
People made the bay this way
so garplegrungen's here to stay!"

The others sadly nodded in agreement, but Chadwick slammed his claw against the ground. "Then we'll have to ask the people to stop putting the garplegrungen into the water!"

Esmerelda gasped. "But we can't *talk* to people!"

"That's right," said Dr. Mallard. "Even if we could talk to people, we couldn't just *ask* them to stop. They've got to pass a law first."

Chadwick turned to Bernie. "What's a law?" he whispered.

"It's like a rule," Bernie said. "People write this rule down on paper and then they vote on whether to keep it or throw it away. If they decide to keep it, then everybody has to do what it says or else they go to jail. That's a law."

"How do we get them to make a law?" Chadwick asked Bernie.

Bernie shrugged and looked at Toulouse. Toulouse shrugged and looked at Baron von Heron. But the Baron had run out of rhymes. Everyone turned to Orville the Oyster, but Orville was just as quiet as ever and Chadwick took that as a bad sign. If Orville didn't know the answer, maybe there was none.

Just then, a cloud of sand bubbled to the surface. Toulouse and Bernie jumped back and Dr. Mallard held a wing over his thumping heart.

"This is it!" Bernie screeched. "The garplegrungen is brewing underneath. It's going to explode, blowing us all to smithereens!"

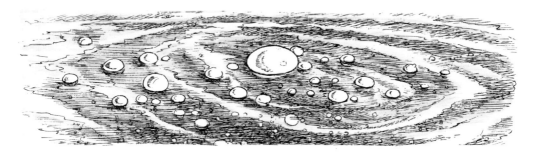

But it was just Belly Jeans shaking himself off.

"Excuse me," the flounder said shyly, "but perhaps we could letter them a write."

"*Letter them a write?!* Hey! Who invited this dumb flounder here?" Bernie squawked with laughter, relieved that they weren't in danger after all.

"Don't laugh, Bernie," Chadwick said. "It's a good idea. What Belly Jeans means is that we could *write the people a letter* and tell them they have to pass a law to stop the garplegrungen!"

There was another flurry of wet sand.

"Wait—Belly Jeans has something more to say," said Chadwick. "Now think before you speak," he instructed the flounder. "Have some self-confidence and maybe it won't come out backwards."

Belly Jeans paused. "I read a book about this once," he began. "Besides a letter, we'll need proof of just how bad the garplegrungen is, and we'll need supporters to convince the people they need to pass this new law."

"Proof? What could we use for proof?" Chadwick asked.

"I could send them some green and purple pastry," Toulouse offered.

"Or we could send pictures of Matilda to show them how sick she is!" Bernie suggested.

"I beg your pardon!" Matilda shrieked. "I'm not posing for any pictures!"

"Oh, come on. You would if it was going to save us all, wouldn't you?" asked Chadwick.

Matilda pulled the blanket close together at her neck. "Well . . . I don't know," she said.

"Of course you would," said Chadwick. "Bernie, take some pictures of Matilda. Toulouse, you figure out how to get some supporters while I start writing this letter."

Toulouse scratched his head. He figured if a dumb flounder could come up with a good idea, then certainly he could.

The Baron held up a wing to announce he would speak.

"This letter is a fine idea,
    but I need an explanation.
    How can a letter be written
    by a lowly bay crustacean?"

Bernie's beak fell open. "*Lowly crustacean?* Now, you wait a minute. Just because Chadwick has a shell doesn't mean he's dumb."

Toulouse agreed. "No, indeed, Your Birdship. Chadwick's not lowly—we think very highly of him, in fact."

Chadwick simply ignored the Baron's remark. He took a pencil and began the letter while Bernie stomped off to look for a camera, mumbling under his breath as he left. "Lowly crustacean. Who does he think he is? Next time, I'll tell that skinny-legged windbag a thing or two."

Chadwick worked on the letter all afternoon. Esmerelda checked it for spelling and grammar and when it was finally finished, Chadwick signed his name and passed it around.

"You can't just sign it 'Chadwick,' " Dr. Mallard said. "You've got to spice it up a little. People always have two names, and most of them have a fancy middle initial."

"Well. All right," said Chadwick. He thought for a minute. "I'll sign it 'Chadwick A. Crab.' "

"Yeah—and I'll be 'Bernard C. Gull!' " Bernie chuckled.

The others added their names, too: B.J. Flounder, Baron Von Heron, S. Merelda Crab, Dr. Mallard Duck, Matilda E. Gret, and Orville N. Oyster.

Chadwick folded the letter. "We've got to get this delivered to the State House right away," he said. "Where are those pictures of Matilda?"

"I'm sorry, Chadwick," said Bernie. "I've looked all through my junk and I just can't find a camera."

Chadwick sighed. "I guess we won't have any proof after all. And since Toulouse has disappeared, there won't be any supporters either. We'll just have to hope this one little letter does some good," he said to Esmerelda as he addressed the envelope to The Peoples' Governor.

"Oh, for goodness sakes, give me that letter," Matilda grumped as she struggled to her feet. "I'll take it to the State House *myself*. Then the people can really see how sick I am."

Chadwick tried to stop her, but it was no use. When Matilda made up her mind to do something, that was it. Dr. Mallard helped Matilda tie on her hat and off she went, wearing the blanket like a cloak and carrying the letter in her bill.

Over the bay she flew and on into town, where she landed with a clumsy thud on the stone-hard State House steps. She took a minute to straighten her hat and smooth her feathers. Then, with her head held high, she walked through the tall doors and went inside the large brick building.

People were so startled to see a long-legged bird in the marble hallways that they moved aside and made way for Matilda. On she went, down the aisle between the lawmakers and up to the big desk, where The Governor stood. Everyone in the crowded room stopped talking. Matilda dropped the letter and then, exhausted from the effort, she fainted.

The people waited silently as The Governor read the letter aloud:

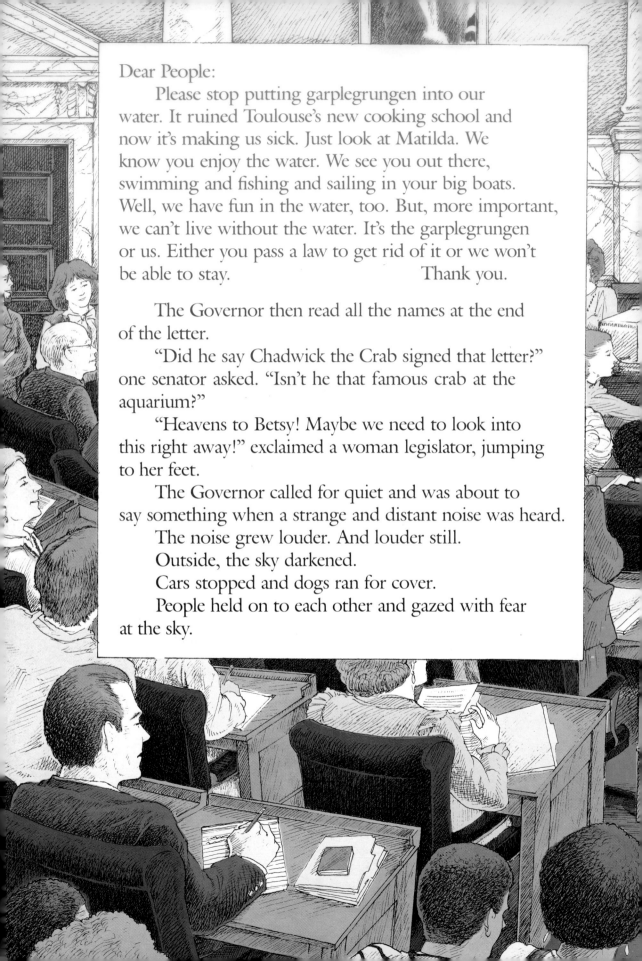

Dear People:

 Please stop putting garplegrungen into our water. It ruined Toulouse's new cooking school and now it's making us sick. Just look at Matilda. We know you enjoy the water. We see you out there, swimming and fishing and sailing in your big boats. Well, we have fun in the water, too. But, more important, we can't live without the water. It's the garplegrungen or us. Either you pass a law to get rid of it or we won't be able to stay.   Thank you.

 The Governor then read all the names at the end of the letter.

 "Did he say Chadwick the Crab signed that letter?" one senator asked. "Isn't he that famous crab at the aquarium?"

 "Heavens to Betsy! Maybe we need to look into this right away!" exclaimed a woman legislator, jumping to her feet.

 The Governor called for quiet and was about to say something when a strange and distant noise was heard.

 The noise grew louder. And louder still.

 Outside, the sky darkened.

 Cars stopped and dogs ran for cover.

 People held on to each other and gazed with fear at the sky.

Suddenly, from behind a cloud, Toulouse appeared, honking triumphantly and leading a large "V" of French Canada geese. Behind him were hundreds of egrets, herons, ducks, sea gulls—and thousands upon thousands of more geese flying, row after row, in "V" formations. Their wings made a thunderous sound as they flew down upon the State House grounds. There were birds everywhere: on statues and on street lights, on mailboxes, cars, bicycles, stair railings—even on baby carriages. Some of the birds, led by Toulouse, marched right inside the State House, filling the hallways with so much honking, quacking, and squawking that nothing else could be heard.

Lawmakers jumped on top of their desks to get out of the way.

"I think we should pass a law immediately!" a man with a bow tie called out.

Another threw up his hand. "I agree! This law certainly has a lot of supporters!"

The Governor called for order. "Quiet!" he hollered. "It's clear we must do something. Without geese and crabs and . . . " He looked at Matilda, who was still sprawled before him, "without egrets too, the bay just wouldn't be the same!"

That very day, the people voted and passed a law that made everyone stop putting the awful garplegrungen in the water. It would take many months—and perhaps years—before the garplegrungen went away completely, but it wasn't long before most of the green and purple bubbles started to disappear.

By spring, when the daffodils were in bloom, Matilda felt better and was her grumpy self again. Dr. Mallard took a vacation because no one was sick, and Toulouse had flown back to Canada with the other geese.

All the crabs had awakened from their winter nap and returned to Shady Creek, where Bug-Eyed Benny said he could really see the difference in the water. Hector Spector the Jellyfish arrived, but couldn't make up his mind whether the water was clearer or not. The Bluefish Patrol was back on duty and Belly Jeans had so much self-confidence that he was writing a book about himself. He was going to call it *Life at the Bottom,* by B.J. Flounder.

It was time, Chadwick decided, to return to Baltimore. "Are you ready?" he called to Esmerelda. Just the night before, with the full moon's silvery light shimmering through the water, Chadwick had asked her to go back to the aquarium with him.

"We'll be seeing you, Bernie. If you're ever up in Baltimore, give us a squawk," Chadwick said, chuckling.

Just then, Baron von Heron strolled in.

"I wonder what his Skinny-leg-ship wants," Bernie muttered.

The Baron cleared his throat—"ahem!"—and said:

"Please pardon me, Chadwick. I do apologize
for calling you lowly when you're quite otherwise.
In fact, I've never met a smarter crab than you!
My thanks for all you've done. Good luck in all you do!"

Bernie ruffled his wing feathers. "Yeah. I agree with ole Rhymin' Simon here."

"That's very nice," Chadwick replied.

"But give credit where it's due.
To keep the water blue, 'tis true,
we all did what we had to do."

And with that he winked at Bernie, took Esmerelda's claw, and kicked off for the long swim back to Baltimore.

90 91 92 7 6 5 4 3